ALIEN ENCOUNTER

SUSANNAH BRIN

Artesian Press
P.O. Box 355 Buena Park, CA 90621

Take Ten Books
Chillers

Other Take Ten Themes:
Mystery
Adventure
Disaster
Sports
Thrillers
Fantasy

Development and Production: Laurel Associates, Inc.
Cover Illustrator:Black Eagle Productions
Cover Designer: Tony Amaro
©2000 Artesian Press

 *Artesian **Press***

ISBN 1-58659-

Contents

Chapter 1

Patches of sunlight danced across the dashboard of Adam Blue's pickup truck as he turned off of the main highway. "Almost there, dudes," Adam announced. Smiling, he gave his friend Leon Ellers an elbow to the ribs.

"I can see that, Blue," answered Leon crossly. He shifted his body, trying to get comfortable. "On the ride back, *I* get the window seat. Sitting in the middle is for the birds."

Charley Parker laughed. "You lost the coin toss, so stop complaining, Leon." Charley rolled his window down and took a deep breath of the crisp mountain air. Grinning at Leon, he leaned back to show that he was as comfortable as a tick on a dog.

"You know it's not right—me sitting in the middle. I'm bigger than you," grumbled Leon. He crossed his huge arms and stared straight ahead.

"You can say that again, Leon. What do you weigh now? Three hundred pounds?" asked Charley, knowing he'd gotten his friend's goat.

"I don't weigh no three hundred pounds," fumed Leon.

"Leave him alone, Charley. The football coach told him to bulk up. He's sure to play varsity at college this fall," explained Blue, an easy smile spreading across his face.

"I didn't know. Congratulations, Leon," said Charley. *"Varsity!* That's really something."

Leon beamed with pride. "Yeah. I was pretty excited when he said that. And old Blue here will probably play second-string quarterback. It's going to be just like it was in high school—except that you won't be there."

Blue drove the pickup through a grove of birch trees and headed north. "I don't understand why you want to go to a college back east. We've got good schools out here. You're breaking up the Three Musketeers, Charley."

Charley laughed. But then he started thinking about all the growing-up years he'd spent with Blue and Leon. They were his best friends. When they were all in grade school, they'd seen the movie, *The Three Musketeers*. Blue had immediately given their group the same name, and it had stuck.

Charley figured he was the only one of them to have actually read the book. He felt bad about leaving. He knew he'd miss them—but his dream was taking him in a different direction. "My dad graduated from Harvard, and he wants me to go there. They've got a great pre-med school."

"You going to med school was not in our plan," muttered Leon, his large handsome face darkening. "We agreed that we'd all go to college together, remember? We'd play football and then get drafted by a professional team."

Charley smiled and looked out the window. A shadow was sliding up the mountain as the sun moved higher in the sky. Charley was more realistic than his friends. He knew he'd never be signed to a pro team. The competition was much too stiff. "I'm just not pro material like you two," he said.

"What are you talking about? You're the fastest runner in the conference. You were named halfback of the year," snorted Blue. "You're making a big mistake. Why anyone would want to be a doctor when he could be playing football is beyond me!"

"Someone has to patch up their broken bones," teased Charley.

Leon nodded. It was easy to get injured playing football. "Okay, so you can be *my* doctor, man. But no shots!"

"It's a deal," laughed Charley, remembering the time in sixth grade when Leon had fainted just from watching Blue get a tetanus shot.

Blue poked at Leon again as he changed the subject. "So, Leon, you didn't answer the question. Do you weigh three hundred pounds or not?"

Leon frowned. "I told you I don't weigh that much. I'm only up to two hundred ninety."

Charley and Blue hooted with laughter.

Leon's frown deepened. "What's so darn funny?"

"*You* are!" laughed Blue. "Shoot, you can add ten pounds just by eating one of your giant snacks."

Leon thought for a moment and then grinned sheepishly. "You're right. But the coach *told* me to bulk up."

"I'll bet he didn't tell you to get up to three hundred pounds. You should try to keep your weight at two hundred sixty or sixty-five. More than that and your heart has to work too hard," counseled Charley.

Leon grinned again. "Look at you. You're doctoring already."

Charley gave him a serious look.

"I know. But not everybody can be a stringbean like you and Blue are," snapped Leon.

"Knock it off, you guys," snapped Blue, pulling the pickup off the road and throwing open the door. "Look! We're here."

"Smell that clean mountain air," said Blue, taking a deep breath. He stretched his long legs and shook some of the kinks from his shoulders.

Leon stretched his arms wide. It looked as if he meant to hug all of the great outdoors.

Charley stared for a long time at the granite-colored Sierra Mountains. They were rugged, harsh in their beauty. Silently, he wondered if the East Coast would have such splendid, rugged mountains—such sprawling wilderness.

Blue began lifting backpacks from the truck's bed. He glanced at his friends. Charley was daydreaming and Leon was finishing off a bag of donuts. "If you want to be fishing by noon, you'd better load up, guys. We've got a two-mile hike up to Gem Lake. That's two miles straight up."

"Why didn't we just go to one of the roadside lakes in Mammoth? No hiking," moaned Leon, squashing the empty donut bag between his hands.

Charley swung his pack onto his back and started buckling the belt. "Quit complaining, Leon. The walk will do you good."

Leon made a face. "Is everyone ready?" asked Blue, raising his fishing pole like a sword.

Leon and Charley laughed, but they raised their poles, too. Then, together, the three boys shouted the Three

Musketeers' rallying cry, *"All for one and one for all!"*

Blue led the way. Charley followed, happy to begin their last adventure together before college. For some unexplainable reason, he felt this would be the adventure they would remember for the rest of their lives.

Chapter 2

Blue led the way up the mountain. Over the years, he had become the unofficial leader of the group. He didn't mind. In fact, he liked thinking up things for them to do. He knew that—left on their own—Leon would veg out in front of the television, and Charley would bury his nose in a book. "You all okay?" he shouted, looking back over his shoulder.

"Yeah," called out Charley and Leon. Leon's voice was strained from breathing hard.

They hiked uphill for an hour. It was a hard climb. The terrain was steep. Sagebrush and dead branches scratched at their bare legs. Rocks of varying sizes slid under their feet, making it more difficult to keep a steady pace. Finally, Leon stopped. He bent over and leaned his hands on his knees, gulping in giant breaths of air.

"Hold up, Blue," hollered Charley, stopping by Leon's side. Charley bent over and looked at Leon with concern.

Blue circled back. "If you did more windsprints at practice, you wouldn't be so out of shape," Blue said, although he, too, was breathing heavily.

Leon reared up like a giant bear and frowned down at Blue, who at five feet, eleven was four inches shorter. "It's hard to breathe up here!" snapped Leon, thinking he was about to have a heart attack. He plopped down on a big rock to rest. Sweat glistened on his face and neck like a smooth sheet of oil.

"It's hard to breathe because the air is thinner up here," Charley explained. Dropping down next to Leon, he was secretly glad for the break.

"Yeah. Why is that?" asked Leon,

relieved to think there wasn't anything wrong with him. But he could still feel his heart pumping hard and fast inside his heaving chest.

"We're more than eight thousand feet above sea level, Leon. The higher you get above sea level, the less oxygen there is in the air. Your lungs have to work harder," explained Charley, sounding like a schoolteacher.

"Working harder is the part that Leon hates," teased Blue. And it was true. Leon didn't like to push himself. In training every year, the coach was always yelling at him to move faster during the warm-up exercises.

"Let's go," said Blue. "It's not much farther to the lake."

"How far?" asked Leon.

Blue rolled his eyes and then looked up at the cloudless blue sky. "I don't know. Maybe a mile."

Leon groaned.

Charley stood and offered his hand

to pull Leon up. "Don't think about it, Leon. Concentrate on putting one foot after the other," he suggested. Then he headed up the trail behind Blue, leaving Leon to bring up the rear.

"Easy for you to say, Charley. You're a beanpole. You don't have my weight to carry," grumbled Leon.

Charley laughed and called over his shoulder, "There *are* advantages to being thin, buddy." When he was younger, he'd hated the nickname *beanpole*, but now the silly name just rolled off his back.

Charley was as tall as Leon, but thinner. And much faster. He could outrun all of his friends without getting winded. The coach had said that one day, he could be the fastest halfback in the NFL. Now he felt a twinge of regret that he was giving up football, but he was determined to become a doctor.

The boys continued on up the mountain. Straggly pines and a few fir trees clung by their roots to the mountainside. A lone hawk slid across the sky, reminding them of balsawood gliders they'd built and flown when they were little boys.

After climbing over a cleft in the mountain, they dropped down into a small meadow of tall grasses and wild flowers. Blue stopped and consulted his map. "We're almost there. The lake is on the other side of that stand of firs," he said, pointing in the direction they were to take.

Leon took off his baseball cap and ran his hand over his short brown hair. The August sun was hot on his face. "Why don't we just camp here?"

"It's too far from the lake," said Blue, not even considering the spot. "Besides, who will keep watch over our stuff when we're fishing if we camp way up here?"

"Jeez, Blue! Who's going to steal our stuff? We haven't seen anyone all afternoon," argued Leon. He wanted to take off his backpack and relax. He was getting tired and hungry, too.

"Well, somebody must have camped here," said Charley, studying the center of the meadow. "Looks like it was a big group, too."

The boys turned and stared at the center of the meadow. The tall grasses and wildflowers were all brown and crushed as if something heavy had sat on them for a while. As they walked closer, they saw that the flattened area was really a huge circle.

"Wow! That must have been some huge tent," exclaimed Leon.

"It was probably more than one," mumbled Blue, not really interested.

"This is really weird," said Charley, a puzzled expression on his face. "Look, everything inside the circle is flat. But the surrounding grasses are undisturbed. It's almost like a helicopter landed here, and no one got out."

"Maybe one landed and took off. *They* probably didn't want to camp here, either. Come on. The sun goes down early up here in the mountains," said Blue. Without waiting for the others, he started for the treeline.

"Must have been a really huge chopper to make a circle that big," said Leon, with a look of awe. Then he turned and followed Blue.

Charley knew that there wasn't a helicopter or a tent large enough to make a circle that big. *What could have created that huge, perfect circle,* he thought to himself *What?*

Chapter 3

After setting up camp, the three friends spent the rest of the afternoon fishing. Leon, tired from the hike, sat on a boulder and dangled his line in the water. Blue and Charley walked the shore as they flyfished. Charley was the first to catch a fish. It was a rainbow trout, small, pan-size—just right for dinner. Minutes later, Blue landed a fifteen-inch trout, the largest catch of the day. Leon didn't get a bite.

As the sun set, long dark shadows spread across the blue-green lake. The temperature fell sharply. Leon shivered and picked up his gear. "Hey, you guys, I'm going back to camp. It's getting awful cold."

"We're coming!" Blue yelled as he reeled in his line. He turned to Charley, who was a few feet away. "Let's pack it in. We need to round up some firewood while there's still enough light to see what we're doing."

Leon grinned. "Why don't you get the fire started while we find more wood? Charley can start the potatoes."

They worked as a team, building the fire and making the dinner. All three of the boys joked and laughed as they worked. After dinner, they stretched out by the campfire.

Using his pack as a pillow, Blue stared up at the night sky. "Boy, you can really see lots of stars up here in the mountains. It's going to be a nice day tomorrow."

Leon glanced at Blue with surprise. "How do you know that?"

"The sky is clear. Look—no clouds," answered Blue.

"Oh," mumbled Leon, looking up again to study the sky.

Charley was lying on top of his sleeping bag with both hands behind his head. He was staring up at the sky, too. But he wasn't thinking about the weather. "I saw a program on television last year. It showed these big flat circles made in some wheat fields in England. The circle up in the meadow made me remember them."

"Yeah? So what were the circles in the wheat all about?" asked Blue.

"No one knows. It's a mystery. Some folks think the circles were made by aliens." Charley smiled, knowing his two friends were going to mock him.

Blue hooted with laughter. *"Aliens? I don't believe you said that. You mean like little green men in a flying saucer?"*

Leon laughed hard, too. Then he pretended to be serious. "Spacemen aren't green. They're the color of flesh, and they have big eyes. Didn't you see the movie *E.T.*?" Both Leon and Blue burst out laughing again.

"You're right, buddy. And in the movie, *Close Encounters of the Third Kind*, they were small with big heads. Just what do *your* aliens look like, Charley?" teased Blue.

Charley threw another log on the fire. He watched as sparks flew up into the night sky like a handful of fireflies released from a bottle. "I don't know what they look like. But it *is* possible that aliens exist, you know."

Blue grinned. "Charley, you've read too many books. Your brain is toast. Even the astronauts haven't seen any aliens—which proves they don't exist."

"That proves nothing. Maybe there is life farther out in the galaxy. Scientists suspect there are living organisms on Mars," argued Charley.

"I heard that, too," offered Leon. "It was on the news. Scientists believe that bacteria are living in the cracks of the rocks brought back from space."

"Well that explains everything," said Blue, shaking his head. His eyes danced with mischief. "We're being invaded by mold men, slime creatures." He waved his arms at Leon as if he was going to shoot him with slime. Leon played along, pretending to be scared.

Charley laughed at their clowning. "Okay, you two. I only said it was a *possibility* that aliens exist." Standing up slowly, he retrieved a big bag of marshmallows from his pack. After sticking one on a pointed stick, he handed the bag to Leon.

"Great idea!" exclaimed Leon, grabbing the bag.

"Go for it, buddy," laughed Charley, roasting his marshmallow. He knew he should change the subject, but he couldn't let it go. "So what do you think made that huge circle up there in the meadow?"

"Beats me," mumbled Leon, his

mouth full of marshmallows.

"It's a freak happening in nature. Or a bunch of insects. Remember in science class how the teacher said a swarm of locusts could eat a whole field of wheat in minutes?" said Blue, thinking the circle was no big deal.

"The grass in the meadow wasn't eaten. It was *flattened*, crushed," answered Charley, rather sharply.

Blue didn't have a comeback. An awkward silence hung in the air.

Blue sat up and looked across the fire at Charley. "Relax, man. We're just teasing. I'll admit that aliens are a possibility. Remember that time in the fifth grade when you froze all those goldfish? You were so positive you could bring them back to life! No one thought you could. But Leon and I agreed to consider the possibility, right? We backed you up."

Charley smiled, remembering. He'd been so *sure* that the goldfish would revive once the ice melted. But they didn't. They just lay dead on top of the ice cube tray. "The experiment didn't work, but I was on the right track. Later I read that to be revived, fish need to be quick-frozen in a special solution."

Leon grinned. "Your experiment stunk up the science lab on Parents' Night. The smell was so bad that my mom hurried out of there so fast she didn't notice that I didn't do a project."

The three old friends talked on until the fire burned low. Finally, Blue yawned and put one last log on the fire. "This should hold us until morning," he said. Then, unzipping his sleeping bag, he crawled in. Leon and Charley did the same.

For a long time, Charley lay awake staring at the night sky, thinking about aliens.

Chapter 4

Sometime in the middle of the night, Charley woke up. The ground was trembling, shaking. He jumped out of his bag and yelled at the others, *"Earthquake!"* Blue woke up with a start and jumped up. He had felt the ground trembling, too.

"Do you feel it?" asked Charley, pulling on his pants.

"Yeah," answered Blue. "I think it's just a small tremor. What are you getting dressed for?"

"What if this is just a warning? A big one could hit at any minute," explained Charley, imagining the ground splitting apart.

"Yeah, right," replied Blue, grabbing his shoes and dressing quickly. "Listen!

What's that sound?"

Charley jerked his head toward Leon. "He's snoring." He kicked Leon's bag a couple of times until his friend woke up.

"Huh? What are you kicking me for?" growled Leon, sitting up and shooting a hard look at Charley.

"We're having an earthquake! Get dressed," Charley snapped, more frightened than angry. "We've got to get to clear ground. I don't want to be here if the trees start falling."

Leon yawned and looked at his two friends as if they had gone crazy. "Is this some kind of a joke? I don't feel a darn thing."

Charley and Blue glanced at each other with surprise. Leon was right. The ground wasn't shaking anymore.

Charley shrugged. "I guess the quake is over," he said.

"I told you it was only a tremor," said Blue.

"When you two figure it out, let me know. Me, I'm going back to sleep," muttered Leon, snuggling down into his sleeping bag. Within seconds, he was snoring again.

Looking at Leon, Charley shook his head. "I don't know how he can fall asleep so easily. I know I won't be able to sleep now."

"Yeah," answered Blue. "There's something about an earthquake that makes me feel all wired—like my energy has kicked into high gear."

Charley stirred the dying embers of the fire. "I get that feeling, too. Sort of edgy. We think we're standing on solid ground. Then along comes a quake and we realize that nothing is solid or permanent. We're powerless against the forces of nature."

"That's a good way of putting it, Charley. We've got all this technology, but we still can't predict an earthquake. It's weird how—"

A deafening boom stopped Blue in midsentence. He jumped to his feet. The noise was so loud that it shook the ground. Leon scrambled from his sleeping bag.

"What was that?" asked Leon. His eyes were wide with fear.

"I don't know," answered Charley. He could feel his heart pumping faster and faster in his chest.

Blue didn't know, either. "It's *huge*, whatever it is."

"Maybe a tree fell?" suggested Leon. "You know—one of those big firs."

"Quiet!" whispered Charley. "I think I hear something."

A humming sound like the whining of a hundred turbo engines filled the silence. The three friends huddled closely together. Fear shone on their faces. They stared up the bank in the direction of the meadow.

"The sound is definitely coming from the meadow," whispered Charley.

"We've got to get out of here," hissed Leon, turning away from the others to grab some of his things.

Charley hurried over to Leon and shook him roughly. "Calm down, man. Panic won't help. I think we should investigate."

Leon stared at Charley as if he'd lost his mind. "No way. Whatever is out there is bigger than we are."

"Look!" said Blue, choked with fear.

Charley and Leon looked in the direction where Blue was pointing. At first, they didn't see anything except the tall, dark shadows of the trees against the night sky.

"What did you see?" asked Charley.

"A beam of light," answered Blue. A minute passed, and then a wide beam of light swept through the trees again. "Did you see that?" he asked.

"It's only a searchlight. Nothing to be scared about," mumbled Leon, trying to put on a brave face.

"Come on. Let's go find out who or what is up there," said Charley, swallowing back his fear.

"You guys go. I'm staying put," said Leon, faking a big yawn as if he felt too sleepy to go along.

"No. We all go together, Leon. We have to remember that we're the Three Musketeers," said Blue. He wasn't too keen on investigating either, but he didn't want Charley to know how he felt. Besides, it was his job as leader to keep them all together.

Leon agreed half-heartedly—just as he usually did when the three of them faced danger or trouble. He would rather fight his battles on the football field. In a way, he was happy that in the fall they'd go their separate ways. Life would be easier then.

Charley started up the bank toward the trees with the other two close behind. He knew his friends were scared. He was, too. But his curiosity was greater than his fear. He thought about the flattened circle up in the meadow. He wondered if what had made that circle was up there now.

Reaching the top of the bank, they crept through the treeline toward the meadow. The humming noise was louder. A thick, heavy mist swirled around their feet and ankles.

"What is this stuff?" asked Blue, looking down at the knee-deep mist.

"I don't know. It's like walking in a cloud," answered Charley, noticing that the mist had risen to his waist.

"I don't like it," complained Leon. He stopped next to Charley and Blue.

"Do you think *we* do?" snapped Blue, his own fear twisting his insides.

Charley stuck out his hand, waiting for them to place their hands on top of his. This was their tradition. Once their hands were on top of each other's, they always whispered the pledge that had kept them together: *"We are the Musketeers. All for one and one for all."*

Then, as a group, they stepped into the meadow. Giant clouds of mist rose up into the sky. The loud humming noise pulsated around them like a giant heartbeat. They walked in the direction of the sound.

"Awesome!" whispered Charley. Surprise and wonderment filled his face as he stared up at a towering, disc-shaped spaceship rising above the mist. Millions of tiny lights winked in the windows of the enormous ship. "Wow! Have you ever seen anything so beautiful in your life?"

Blue and Leon didn't answer. They were speechless.

Against their will, like dream-walkers, the boys were pulled closer and closer to the ship. Then clouds of mist swirled around them, separating them from one another.

Chapter 5

Charley could feel his body being pulled forward. He tried to turn back, but the suction pulling him was too strong. *Might as well go with the flow,* he told himself, knowing that he had no other choice. He swallowed hard. Fear screamed out in his head. Nothing in his life had prepared him for what was happening—not movies, not books, not even his own imaginings.

"Blue! Leon! Where are you?" yelled Charley, feeling more alone than ever.

Blue and Leon didn't answer. But hundreds of high-pitched voices did. The voices chanted, "Blue, Leon, Blue, Leon," as if they were trying out the words. Charley felt the hairs on the back of his neck begin to rise.

Suddenly, the mist cleared a bit and the pulling motion stopped. Charley found himself standing in front of what looked like a door that led into the spacecraft. He glanced around. Blue and Leon were nowhere in sight. He stared up at the silver ship studded with twinkling lights. It was as tall as a New York skyscraper.

"Please enter," said a hollow, computer-like voice.

Charley didn't move. The last thing he wanted to do was enter the ship. *Terrible things could happen to me inside the ship*, he thought. Standing his ground, he didn't move.

"Nothing terrible will happen to you," said the strange, hollow voice. "Please enter now."

"It must have read my mind!" whispered Charley to himself.

"We will help you," said the hollow voice. Then Charley was lifted on a current of air and swept into the spaceship. The air current deposited him in the center of a huge room.

Bright lights blinded him. Charley squinted as he looked around. Beyond the lights he could just make out rows and rows of seats rising in columns toward the ceiling. The floor beneath his feet started to turn slowly. *I must be in some kind of theater*, he thought to himself.

Again, the hollow voice read his mind. "Yes—but we like to call it our viewing room."

Charley swiveled his head in the direction of the voice. But he couldn't see anyone. "Who are you?" he asked. He could hear the shifting of bodies and the sound of excited whispering coming from the rows of seats.

"We are explorers from the LOKI-7 Galaxy. A galaxy many light years from yours," explained the hollow voice.

"What is it you want?" asked Charley, hoping the fear he was feeling didn't make him look weak.

The hollow voice sounded amused as it responded. "That depends on what we find. As I've said, we are explorers. Our mission is to seek out new worlds and observe them."

"That sounds harmless," Charley said guardedly. "Where are my friends, Blue and Leon?"

"They are in our duplicating room," answered the voice.

Charley's heart jumped and raced crazily. The picture of his friends being fed into some kind of weird Xerox machine filled his mind with horror.

The hollow voice chuckled. "Your imagination is running wild again." The unseen audience giggled.

Charley wasn't reassured. Since leaving the campsite, nothing was as it seemed. Besides, he couldn't stop worrying about his buddies. "I can't help what I imagine!" snapped Charley.

"Ah, yes. That is a fault of you

humans. Your mind control is not fully developed like ours. In our duplicating room, we are able to make an exact copy of anything we want. It is a speeded-up version of your earthly cloning projects. Right now we are cloning your two friends," explained the hollow voice.

"Why?" squeaked Charley, his voice shaking with terror.

"We need specimens, examples, to take back to the Supreme Ruler of our galaxy. We've tried before to take humans back with us. Unfortunately, they've all died on the way. Humans age too quickly, you see."

Charley was about to ask another question when he felt a light spray of liquid hit his feet and ankles. "Hey, what is this? What are you doing to me?" he cried, raising his arms to shield his face from the spray. But there was no escaping. The spray continued up his body, drenching him with liquid.

The liquid felt like water, but he couldn't be sure. When he was finally wet from top to bottom, the spraying stopped. Trembling with fury, Charley shook the strange liquid from his hair like a wet dog.

"That was just a disinfectant. Nothing for you to be alarmed about," explained the hollow voice.

"But *why?*" yelled Charley.

A sound like a giant sigh floated across the room. Then the hollow voice said, "You humans are so tiring. Always asking, why, why, why?"

"Well?" said Charley, stubbornly. He wanted an answer.

"My fellow explorers would like to step closer—get in touching range. But your human skin is filled with microscopic bugs that could be harmful to us. So we had to disinfect you."

"Just like doctors scrubbing before an operation?" asked Charley.

"That is correct," answered the flat,

computer-like voice.

The lights that had been blinding Charley were suddenly switched off. He looked out into the darkness, speechless. Slipping off their seats and floating toward him were several hundred space creatures. The tiny creatures reminded him of the cartoon character, Casper the Friendly Ghost. Their little bodies glowed like pearls. Their eyes were round and seemed to glow with an electric blue color.

When the first group of creatures reached him, Charley shrank back.

"Don't be alarmed. I will not hurt you," said one of the creatures as it floated in front of his face. Then, slowly and very softly, the creature touched Charley's cheek.

Charley relaxed. The creature's touch felt good—almost soothing. Then all the creatures were fluttering around him, examining him, touching him. He felt like he was standing in a cloud of butterflies. Feelings of wonder and happiness filled him. *This is like being in a dream*, he thought to himself.

"What is a dream?" boomed the strange hollow voice, startling Charley back to reality.

The creatures retreated and hovered in the air around him. They stared at him with intense curiosity.

For a moment, Charley didn't know what to say. "A dream is something that usually happens when a person is asleep. It can be a bunch of images and feelings, or a storylike happening, or a combination of the two," explained Charley, thinking hard. "Dreams are like weird movies you see when you are asleep. I could be asleep right now and this could all be a dream."

"I see," said the hollow voice. "Then perhaps it is."

The tiny creatures murmured in agreement.

Then, from the back of the dark room came a ten-foot-tall creature. Except for its size, it looked exactly like the tiny creatures. Charley sucked in his breath, seeing the huge creature approach.

The towering creature smiled at Charley. When it spoke, it was with the hollow voice that he had been hearing all along. "Now it is time to take *you* to the duplication room. After that you will be reunited with your friends."

Panicked, Charley's eyes darted about the viewing room, madly looking for a way out.

Sensing his wish to flee, the tiny creatures expanded until they were ten feet tall, too. They formed a tight circle around Charley.

Charley's heart sank as he stared up at the creatures. *They don't look so friendly now*, he thought, realizing there was no way to escape.

Chapter 6

Charley felt himself being pulled down a long hallway. He tried to look around, but his view was blocked by the aliens surrounding him. At the end of the hall, a door swooshed open. Charley was pushed inside.

The room was like a huge glass box. He could see the aliens watching him outside the glass. They were tiny again, their bubble-like faces pressing against the glass wall. "Where am I?" he asked.

"You are in the duplicating room," answered the hollow-voiced alien.

"Who is speaking?" asked Charley. "Why can't I see you?"

The group of aliens at the window parted. The ten-foot-tall creature bent down and looked in the window. "I am the Commander. I have been speaking with you since you entered the craft." Suddenly, the tall creature changed size, becoming as small as the others. He looked exactly the same, except that his blue eyes had stars in them.

"Tell me! Where are my friends, Leon and Blue?" Charley had a terrible feeling something bad had already happened to them.

The Commander snapped his fingers. Again, the crowd parted, allowing four tall aliens to bring in Leon and Blue. "Here are your friends. May we proceed now?"

"Hey, guys. How you doing?" asked Charley, grinning. He'd never been so happy to see his friends. Blue and Leon didn't answer. They didn't smile. They just stared straight ahead like zombies. "What's wrong with them? What did you do?" yelled Charley.

"They are, ah, dreaming," said the Commander with a smile. The tiny aliens giggled at their leader's joke.

Charley felt his body begin to shake. *They're going to make me a zombie too*, he thought. He glanced at the sealed door. He was in a glass cage!

"You cannot escape. But what is a *zombie*?" asked the Commander.

"It's a person who acts like a robot. A person who has fallen under a spell," explained Charley.

"You earthlings have such wild imaginations! No wonder you are so often frightened by things you do not understand or cannot explain. Enough talk. It is time to begin," said the Commander. "Stand completely still."

Charley tried, but his legs shook.

"Stop that shaking," ordered the Commander.

"I can't," said Charley, getting angry in spite of himself.

One of the aliens whispered to the Commander, who nodded in reply. "You are like your friends. They could not stand still, either. Get the restraints."

Before Charley could protest, tiny ropes the size of spiderwebs gripped his arms and legs. He felt himself being stretched and pulled until he couldn't move a muscle.

A bright purplish light came on inside the glass cage. Charley felt something pierce his neck. It was as if the light was pulsing inside him like an extra heartbeat. He heard a whirring sound. As the sound got louder, the purplish light grew brighter and hotter. Then, when Charley thought that he couldn't stand it anymore, everything stopped. Again, he felt a piercing sensation as something exited from his neck behind his left ear. Then he felt the restraints falling from his body.

"Now, that wasn't so bad, was it?" asked the Commander, looking closely at Charley.

"No," answered Charley. He rubbed the spot behind his left ear.

The Commander nodded. "The pain will go away. Unfortunately, our cloning light left you with a tiny blue scar behind your ear."

Charley continued to rub at the stinging spot. "Great. Just what I wanted—a tattoo."

"I'm sorry. It couldn't be helped. It is our way of tagging species we have cloned. I believe that you humans do something similar to animals and other wildlife you are studying."

"Yes, but only so we can study them. Some of the animals we study are endangered species," explained Charley, irritably.

"Exactly what we are doing," smiled the Commander.

"*Humans* aren't an endangered species," snapped Charley. He resented being compared to an animal.

"Not at this time—but one never knows what your future will bring. Your planet is in trouble. There is a hole in the ozone. Your energy sources are less than they were. You and your kind contaminate the land daily," answered the Commander.

Charley didn't want to have a conversation with the Commander. He wanted to get out of there.

"Yes, you can go now," said the Commander, reading Charley's mind. "Perhaps we will meet again."

Within seconds, Charley felt himself being shoved from the spaceship. Before he knew it, he landed flat on his back in the meadow.

As the door of the giant ship began to close, he saw both Leon and Blue standing inside. Next to them was a carbon copy of himself.

Chapter 7

Charley glanced around. He couldn't see anything except the clouds of mist spewing from the bottom of the spacecraft. He stared up at the giant ship as its engines revved louder. Slowly, it began to rise. "Incredible," he muttered to himself. The mist swirled around him. He coughed, then turned and ran in the direction of the campsite.

As he ran, the ground trembled and shook as the spaceship lifted off. Charley glanced over his shoulder. The ship was already thrusting out into space at an incredible speed. The ship's burners sucked up the misty clouds into the night sky.

If I didn't know better, I wouldn't believe a spaceship had ever landed here,"

Charley thought to himself.

Crashing through the trees and brush, Charley ran as fast as he could. "Blue! Leon! Hey, guys!" he yelled, praying that they had made it back to camp and were waiting for him, safe and sound.

When he got to the camp, he saw that his two friends were sleeping. He whooped with delight.

"Why are you making so darn much noise?" snarled Leon, sitting up in his sleeping bag. He rubbed his eyes and shot Charley an irritated look.

"Yeah, pipe down!" grumbled Blue. "You'll wake up the fish."

"I don't care. I'm just so happy to see you two. I thought the commander of the spaceship might have lied to me. I thought he'd taken you both back to LOKI-7 Galaxy," explained Charley, grinning with relief.

Blue glanced at Leon, then stared up at Charley as if he were crazy.

"Slow down, buddy. Did you say *spaceship?*" asked Blue.

"Yeah, that's what I said," answered Charley. "You know—the spaceship we were all in just a while ago."

Leon shook his head and rolled his eyes. "*Now* I've heard everything. That was some dream you had, Charley." Leon laughed, then snuggled back down into his sleeping bag.

"Don't go back to sleep, Leon! It *wasn't* a dream—*really*! We were in a spaceship. Don't you remember? We thought there was an earthquake. Then Blue saw a searchlight and we all went up to the meadow to investigate. We got separated in those clouds of mist," said Charley, speaking as fast as he could.

"The only thing I remember is going to sleep. And I was having a good snooze until you woke me up just now," grumbled Leon. He pulled the sleeping bag up around his ears and closed his eyes again.

Frustrated, Charley turned to Blue, who was now sitting up and poking at the dead fire. "*You* remember, don't you, Blue?"

Blue shook his head. "Like Leon, the last thing I remember is falling asleep." Realizing that Charley was very upset, Blue tried to calm him down. "I think you had a bad dream. Before you fell asleep you were talking about that darned circle up in the meadow and some circles you'd seen on television. That's probably why you dreamed that you saw a spaceship."

"I *did* see a spaceship. *I went in it*— just like you and Leon. We didn't have any choice," argued Charley.

"Right. And we chatted with little green men about their home in outer space," said Blue sarcastically.

"They weren't green. They were

white. They reminded me of Casper the Friendly Ghost. You know, that cartoon character?" argued Charley.

Blue nodded and said wearily, "I know who Casper is. Look, Charley, your aliens can look like whatever you want. It's *your* dream, okay?"

Anger flared in Charley's chest. "If I was dreaming, how come I'm up and dressed? And how come I just came back from the meadow?"

"Sleep walking?" suggested Blue with a yawn. "Come on, Charley, go on to bed now. It's going to be light in another hour or so."

"Yeah, okay. We can talk about what happened in the morning," agreed Charley, knowing he wasn't going to convince Blue of anything. He watched Blue lie back down and close his eyes. Soon his friend was fast asleep. Charley shook his head. He couldn't believe it. His friends didn't remember a thing. *Did I dream the whole thing?* he wondered as he flopped down on his sleeping bag.

No, I was there! *Inside the spaceship,* he told himself. He lay back on his bag and stared up at the sky. It looked the same as it always had. Millions of stars winked in the inky blackness. He searched the sky for the spaceship. But the only moving object he saw was an airplane headed south toward Los Angeles.

Charley was too keyed up to sleep. He watched the sun come up over the mountains. When it was light enough to see, he headed back up the bank to the meadow.

The meadow glistened with dew. It looked serene, peaceful. Charley took a deep breath. Hazy images of the night before flashed through his head. He realized that the encounter was slowly slipping from his mind. It was as if the memory of the incident was being erased from his mind. *Maybe that's what happened to Leon and Blue*, he thought. *The incident faded from their minds when they went to sleep.*

Charley had to admit it. In the morning light, the whole thing did seem more like a dream. Yet doubts still filled his mind. He walked toward the spot where he'd seen the spacecraft. The huge circle of flattened grasses and weeds was still there. *At least I didn't dream up this circle*, he thought, feeling a bit of relief.

Charley studied the circle, looking for clues, for something left behind. But the only thing he could find was a rusted bottlecap.

"Hey, Charley, breakfast is ready, man!" yelled Blue, stepping out of the treeline into the meadow.

"Great!" answered Charley, trying to think of a way to convince his friends that a spaceship had really landed—and that the three of them had been cloned.

Chapter 8

Over breakfast, Charley tried to talk to his friends about the spaceship. He went over all the things that had happened, starting with the ground trembling. Blue and Leon couldn't even remember that. Charley tried to think of something that would prove it to them. He had a nagging suspicion that he was forgetting something important—something that couldn't help but convince his friends.

"Give it a rest, Charley," snapped Blue, picking up his fishing pole. "We've got some serious fishing to do."

"Yeah, and I'm going to hook the big one today," bragged Leon, grinning from ear to ear.

"How are you going to do that,

Leon—wrestle the fish to shore?" teased Charley, dropping the subject of the aliens. He knew he couldn't convince them until he remembered more of what had happened.

Leon grinned, already thinking of a retort. "I may not be the best fisherman, but at least I don't have weird dreams like you. We should call you *Yoda* after that strange-looking character in one of the *Star Wars* movies."

Blue frowned. "Come on, you two. This is our last day together. Let's make the most of it."

Charley and Leon grinned at each other. Then they turned wide eyes on Blue, as if they were innocent of any mischief or wrongdoing.

Blue laughed and shook his head. "I'm going upstream, and then I'll work my way back down."

"Sounds good to me," said Charley, following Blue along the rocky edge of the riverbank.

"I'm going to sit right there on that boulder and wait for you," said Leon, pointing to a giant rock in the river.

"If you get any lazier, Leon, you'll be dead," teased Blue. He and Charley headed up the river.

"So make fun. Go right ahead—but you won't be laughing so hard when I land a fifteen-pound brown trout," yelled Leon.

"He might, too," laughed Charley.

"He'll catch a fish that's as lazy as he is," joked Blue.

They walked past the swift-moving rapids to a spot where the river widened and slowed to an easy current. Charley began rigging his pole.

"I'm going up a few yards to get out of your way," said Blue. "What kind of fly are you going to use?"

"A blue meany," answered Charley, holding up a tiny furry-looking bug.

"I can't believe you still have that one. Wasn't that the first fly we ever made?" asked Blue in surprise.

"It was. Remember how Leon's fly had so much glue on it, it looked like a gumball?" said Charley, laughing.

"He never did get the hang of making flies. The guy's just got no patience." Blue grinned, but then he quickly turned serious. "I'm really going to miss spending time with you, buddy."

Charley cast his line across the river. The fly skittered on the water like a real bug. "I'll miss you, too. But it's not like I'm going to another planet." Charley shot a quick glance at Blue, but his friend didn't react. "I'll be home on holidays, you know."

"I know, but it won't ever be the same. The Three Musketeers are busting up," said Blue, his eyes watching his own line skim lightly across the top of the river.

"Yeah," agreed Charley. Together,

they fished away the morning. They each got a few bites, but neither caught anything. The sun was high overhead when they went downstream and found Leon perched on his boulder.

"I don't know why we haven't caught anything," grumbled Blue. "The fish were really biting last night."

"Charley's aliens probably spooked them," teased Leon.

"Yeah, maybe the aliens sucked all the fish up out of the river when they blasted off," added Blue, his eyes dancing with laughter.

Charley didn't say anything. He just shook his head.

Leon scratched at a spot behind his left ear. "I wish they would have taken all the mosquitoes with them, too."

"I'm with you on that, Leon. The one that bit me must've been as big as a bee. I have a bite behind my ear that must be the size of a walnut," said

Blue, rubbing at the sore, itchy spot.

"Let's get some lunch. I'm starving," said Charley.

"Charley, did the mosquitoes get you last night?" asked Leon.

"No," answered Charley.

Blue rubbed the spot behind his ear again. "Sure is odd that the mosquitoes got us both behind the left ear."

A flashbulb went off in Charley's head. *That's IT! My proof*, he thought to himself. "Here—let me see," he said. He checked the spot behind Blue's ear, and then Leon's. Each boy had the same small blue tattoo mark.

"Were we all bit by some strange mosquito that carries a deadly disease?" asked Leon, looking suddenly nervous.

"No," answered Charley, "We were *cloned*. Look, I've got the same bite. Except it isn't a bite. It's more like a tattoo." Before his friends could speak, Charley explained how they'd been cloned by the aliens.

As Blue and Leon listened, they both rubbed the spot behind their ears. Charley could see by the expressions on their faces that they were still skeptical.

"I don't know," said Blue, not quite buying Charley's story.

"How do you smart guys explain the coincidence, then?" asked Charley.

Blue frowned. "I can't."

"You mean there are carbon copies of the three of us out there in space somewhere?" asked Leon, starting to believe Charley.

"Yes," said Charley.

"Here, let me look," said Blue, stepping over to Charley and looking behind his left ear. He looked at Leon's tattoo, as well. Then, using a mirror, he looked at his own blue spot.

"We'll have to take your word, Charley. There's no explaining how we all got tattooed in the night. It *must* have been aliens."

"Wow!" exclaimed Leon. "And I

can't even remember it."

"It's what you get for being so concerned about your beauty rest," teased Charley, glad that his friends finally believed him.

"I guess this means that the Three Musketeers won't ever be separated," said Blue in a serious, thoughtful voice.

The three boys looked at each other and grinned.

"Well, our *clones* won't be, that's for sure," answered Charley.

The three friends grinned. They looked up at the cloudless blue sky. Somewhere beyond their galaxy, the Three Musketeers would live on forever.